D1222288

Beaver,
Bear,
Snowshoe
Hare

North Woods Mammal Poems

By Cheryl Dannenbring
Illustrations by Anna Hess

Raven Productions, Inc.
Ely, Minnesota

What are those funny names?

Felidae

Canidae

Scientists sort animals into large groups with similar characteristics. They call these groups *families*. Here are the family names for the mammals in this book. They may look funny to you because they are Latin names. Each animal also has a two-part name, a *genus* and a *species*, which you can find on the poetry pages.

Cervidae

Cervidae

Bovidae

Leporidae

Soricidae

Ursidae

MAMMAL

Vespertilionidae

Mustelidae

Sciuridae

Why have such complicated names? Good question. People who study animals come from many different countries and speak different languages. Even people who speak the same language might use different **common names** for the same animal.

Mustelidae

Castoridae

For instance, in the United States and Canada some people call an Eastern Fox Squirrel (*Sciurus niger*) a Red Squirrel, and in some places a Red Squirrel (*Tamiasciurus hudsonicus*) might be called a Pine Squirrel or a Chickaree. Confusing, isn't it? However, people using the **scientific names** — the genus and species — know exactly which squirrel they are talking about.

Mustelidae

You can have fun learning the scientific names of plants and animals. Find a teacher who will help you figure out how to pronounce them, then impress your friends and parents.

Dipodidae

Talpidae

TAXONOMY

Erethizontidae

What makes a poem?

The poems in this book look and sound different from the information paragraphs because they *are* different! Poems use more than the meaning of words; they use the sound of words and even how the words look on the page. Many poems have rhythm and rhyme. Like music, they can be heard or read again and again, and still be fun. These poems are meant to make you giggle, gasp, or say "Wow!" Sometimes they follow a special pattern. Here are some of the poetry forms you will find in this book:

Cumulative poems accumulate as the lines from the previous verses are repeated and new lines are added. One of the best-known cumulative poems is "The House that Jack Built."

Free verse poems do not use a regular rhyming or rhythmic pattern, freeing the poet to try new ways of putting sounds and rhythms together.

Haiku is an old form of Japanese poetry. In English, Haiku is written in three lines using 17 syllables or fewer (5-7-5 or short-long-short). Sometimes haiku is written like a riddle that the reader can try to solve.

Limericks are funny and fun to write. They all follow the same pattern: three beats in the 1st, 2nd, and 5th lines, which rhyme; and two beats in the 3rd and 4th lines, which also rhyme. The last line is the punch line.

Lullabies are sung to children to help them fall asleep. The lullaby at the end of this book still needs a tune.

Lyrics are the words written for a song. Some lyrics are lullabies.

Narrative poems tell a story that can be short or long. They usually have a rhythm and a rhyme pattern that is repeated throughout.

Pantoums have a tricky repetition pattern. The second and fourth line of one verse become the first and third line of the next verse. Finally, the last line has to be the same as the first. Every other line rhymes.

Sonnets have fourteen lines and a set rhyming pattern. Often there is a change in mood after the first eight lines and two rhyming lines at the end.

Villanelles always have nineteen lines. There are five verses with three lines and a final verse of four lines. Two lines repeat themselves throughout the poem. The end rhymes also repeat.

Syllabic verse has lines that mirror themselves as the poem progresses. For example, if the first line has 2 syllables, the second has 5, and the third has 7, then the fourth line has 7, the fifth has 5 and the sixth is back down to 2. There is no limit on the number of lines, and the poem may rhyme or not.

Arctic Shrew

Come on down to the swamp café!
Breakfast, lunch, dinner —
   we're open all day.
Centipede feet, earthworm stew,
   gourmet treats
   for an Arctic Shrew.
Eat up quick
   and come back soon.
Hungry again at half-past noon?
Sip a slug shake
   for a picker-upper,
And don't be late
   for our caterpillar supper!

Sorex arcticus

Arctic Shrews weigh only half
as much as a common house mouse,
but they dine on everything served at the
Swamp Café. Since they do not hibernate, they must eat
many times a day just to keep themselves alive, especially during
cold winter months. Your heart beats about 100 times per minute,
but an Arctic Shrew's heart beats about 1200 times each minute.
It takes a lot of energy to keep that ticker ticking!

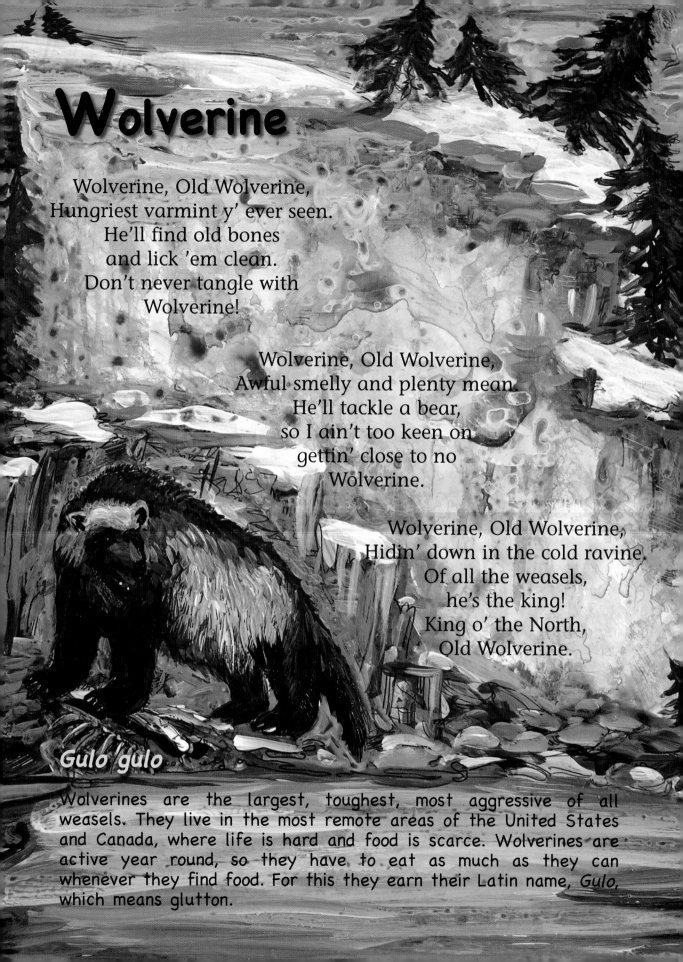

Wolverine

Wolverine, Old Wolverine,
Hungriest varmint y' ever seen.
He'll find old bones
and lick 'em clean.
Don't never tangle with
Wolverine!

Wolverine, Old Wolverine,
Awful smelly and plenty mean.
He'll tackle a bear,
so I ain't too keen on
gettin' close to no
Wolverine.

Wolverine, Old Wolverine,
Hidin' down in the cold ravine.
Of all the weasels,
he's the king!
King o' the North,
Old Wolverine.

Gulo gulo

Wolverines are the largest, toughest, most aggressive of all weasels. They live in the most remote areas of the United States and Canada, where life is hard and food is scarce. Wolverines are active year round, so they have to eat as much as they can whenever they find food. For this they earn their Latin name, *Gulo*, which means glutton.

Pine Marten

under the tree lies
a tiny pile of white bones
fox face high above

Haiku

Martes americana

Pine Martens are members of the weasel family.
They are shy creatures and prefer forests with
heavy undergrowth where they can hide and
make their dens. They have fox-like faces, and
their fur is a reddish brown. They are good
climbers. If you glance up and think you see a
fox in a tree, it's probably a Pine Marten.

Woodland Caribou

Deep in the North Woods,
  a long time ago,
Long before Arctic Cats
  ran through the snow,
Lived herds of deer,
  the whole woodland through,
Deer with big antlers we call Caribou.

Caribou loved winters wild and cold,
Safe in their forests,
  so deep and so old.
When snow drifted up to their
  knobbly knees,
They'd munch on the lichen
  that hung from the trees.

Caribou wandered
  and Caribou played,
But new folk came north,
  and they chopped, and they stayed
'Til every tall tree many miles around
Shivered and timbered
  and fell to the ground.

Forests once quiet
  had roads winding through 'em;
Then lots of cabins
  and roads leading to 'em.
Caribou found it much harder to hide,
Now that their home
  had these people inside!

If you go north now,
 just look far and near,
You'll see lots of mooses
 and white-tailed deer,
But only the lucky and only a few
Ever will see a north woods Caribou.

Rangifer tarandus

When old-growth forests are damaged by human activity, Woodland Caribou lose one of their primary sources of food: the lichens that grow only on very old trees. Deer and moose move into the thinned forests, and Woodland Caribou get pushed out. They are now one of the most endangered mammals of North America.

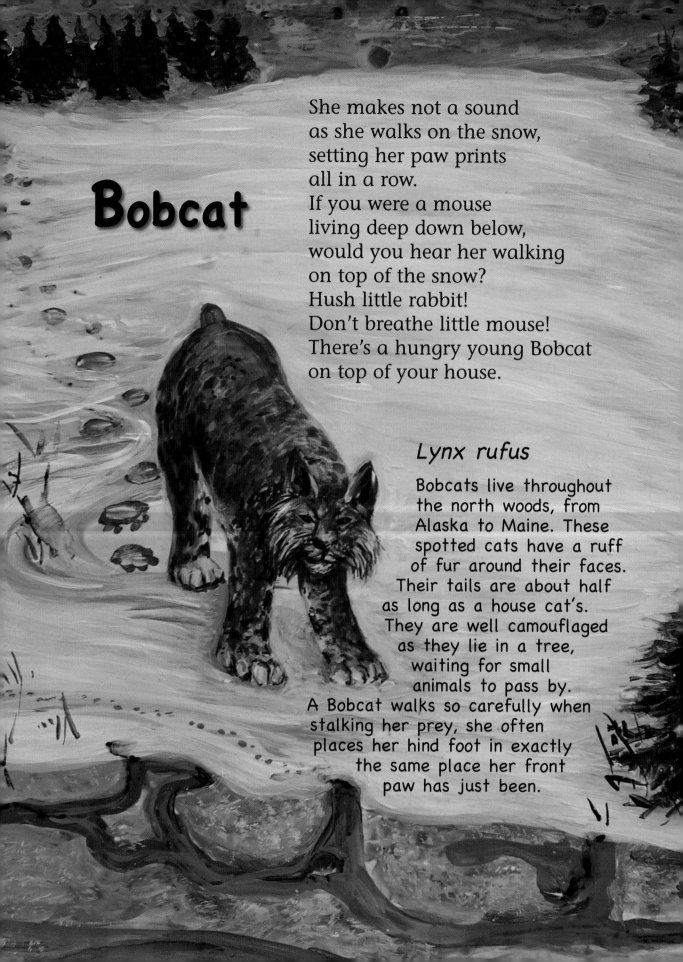

Bobcat

She makes not a sound
as she walks on the snow,
setting her paw prints
all in a row.
If you were a mouse
living deep down below,
would you hear her walking
on top of the snow?
Hush little rabbit!
Don't breathe little mouse!
There's a hungry young Bobcat
on top of your house.

Lynx rufus

Bobcats live throughout
the north woods, from
Alaska to Maine. These
spotted cats have a ruff
of fur around their faces.
Their tails are about half
as long as a house cat's.
They are well camouflaged
as they lie in a tree,
waiting for small
animals to pass by.
A Bobcat walks so carefully when
stalking her prey, she often
places her hind foot in exactly
the same place her front
paw has just been.

Snowshoe Hare

Oh yes!
I can leap —
quick as the wink of an eye —
twelve feet over the deep
and glistening snow.
But for now, I think,
I'll just lie low.

Lepus americanus

Instead of trying to outrun
predators like their larger hare
cousins, Snowshoes often lie
still, trying not to be seen.
As days grow shorter towards
winter, Snowshoes turn from
brown to white. This provides
great camouflage when
snow covers the ground.
But if the snows don't come,
a little white hare is "easy
pickins" for Bobcats and
owls, even at night.

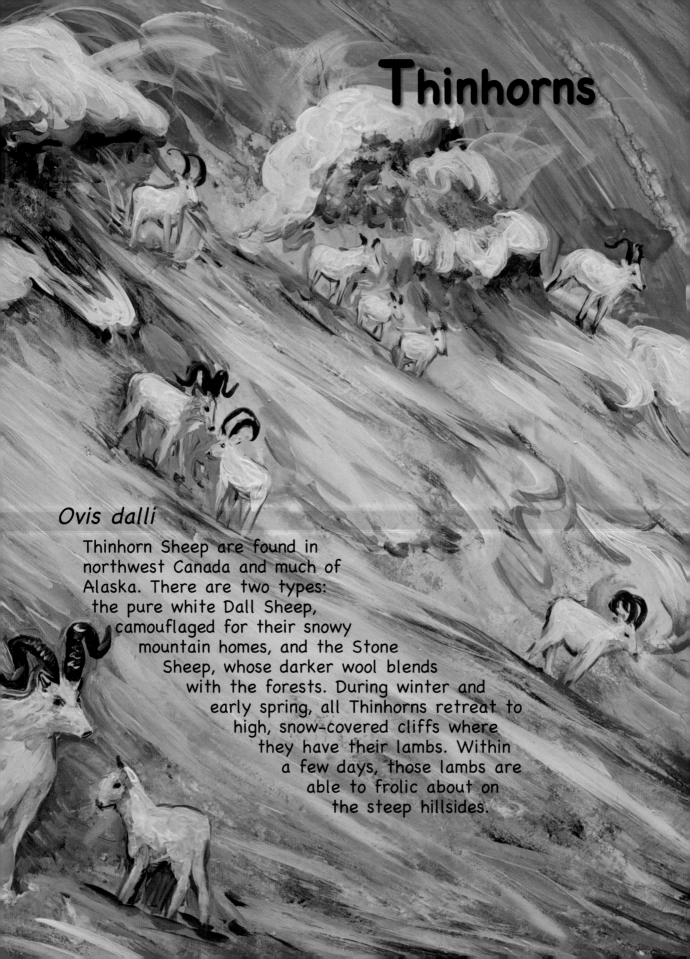

Thinhorns

Ovis dalli

Thinhorn Sheep are found in northwest Canada and much of Alaska. There are two types: the pure white Dall Sheep, camouflaged for their snowy mountain homes, and the Stone Sheep, whose darker wool blends with the forests. During winter and early spring, all Thinhorns retreat to high, snow-covered cliffs where they have their lambs. Within a few days, those lambs are able to frolic about on the steep hillsides.

We're Thinhorns with big horns
   and a thick thatch of wool,
We thrive in a throng
   through the sleet and the snow.
We're Thinhorns with thick horns
   that spiral and curl.
Our coats are too thrummy
   for sharp winds to thirl.
With a thump and a thud
   our rams threaten and threap
While hither and thither
   they bound and they leap.
It's thrilling, though chilling,
   when blizzard winds blow.
To thrive we must thrash
   to the thatch through the snow.
We're Thinhorns with big horns
   now thirsty and lean.
We're thinking and dreaming
   of grass thick and green.
When warm thermals thaw us
   and give us a thrill,
We nimbly-thimbly
   thunder downhill!

Beaver

Castor canadensis

If you saw a Beaver's teeth up close, you might think they needed a good brushing! Our teeth's enamel contains calcium, which makes them white, but the enamel on Beavers' teeth contains iron. The iron turns their teeth orange, but makes them extra strong. A Beaver's teeth keep growing year after year, so he can just gnaw, and gnaw, and gnaw! (On trees, that is ... just kidding about the cake.)

Billy Beaver from Devilfish Lake
Developed an awful toothache.
    He had gum disease,
    And it hurt to gnaw trees,
So his mom made him marshmallow cake.

Limerick

Moose

Alces alces

Moose are the biggest members of the deer family in the whole world. They like to live in wooded areas near water, where they can peacefully munch on waterlilies and willow. But beware! A moose can swim at six miles per hour, so you can't out-swim him. He can run through the woods at thirty miles per hour, so you sure can't out-run him. Better just give him lots of room.

Hey
Mikey Moose
is on the loose.
His hair is brown, his eyes are puce.
He's twice as big as a caboose!
Make way! Make way!
for Mikey
Moose.

Syllabic verse

Gray Wolf

You all know the story
   of Red Riding Hood,
that sweet little child
   who got lost in the wood,
but you're sadly misled
if it brings fear and dread
of the wolf, the noble Gray Wolf!

Miss Hood lost her bearings
   because she forgot
to carry her compass
   each time she went out.
So she sat on the ground
until she was found
by the wolf, the intelligent Wolf!

Canis lupus

The Gray Wolf is given a bad rap in many folk tales. Real wolves live in family groups called packs, with leaders known as the alpha male and alpha female. Only the alpha pair have offspring. Other adults work

Now a wolf knows the woods
  like the back of his paw.
He led her to Granny's
  in no time at all.
He just stayed for tea,
If you don't believe me,
  ask the wolf, the sociable Wolf!

The story was twisted,
  embellished with lies.
Could a real wolf dress-up
  in Granny disguise?
And oh, what a shame
to spoil the good name
of the wolf,
  the noble Gray Wolf!

Narrative

cooperatively to raise the pups and hunt.
When wolves hunt large animals, like deer
or moose, they often kill the sick or weak
ones. We call this "survival of the fittest"
and it helps keep the herds healthy. Wolves
are important members of their ecosystems!

Star-nosed Mole

We are the Shunned Ones,
The Hidden Ones,
Burrowing
Under the
Flora,
Subterranean
Insectivora.
We are the Black Ones,
The Velvet Ones,
Tunneling deep
Through the
Night,
Never seeking the
Light.
We are the Insect Eaters,
The Pest Defeaters,
Equipped for Earthworm
Detection
With Twenty-two
Tentacled
Muzzle
Projections.
We are the Ugly Ones,
The Clawed Ones.
We are the Shunned Ones,
The Hidden Ones.
We are the
Moles!

Free verse

Condylura cristata

Star-nosed Moles spend most of their lives in their tunnels. They eat worms, grubs, underwater bugs and, being good swimmers, even small fish. When hunting, the Star-nose's extremely sensitive tentacles are always moving, but when she eats, she clumps them together to get them out of the way.

Jumping Mouse

Little Mouse, in the wood so deep,
how carefully you walk.
Why don't you **L E A P** ?

    At that slow speed, how will you keep
    safe from the owl and hawk?
    Little Mouse, the wood is so deep,

and your enemies are not asleep.
Nighttime is their time to stalk.
Why don't you **L E A P** and **L E A P** ?

    To safety, leap!
    Do not stop to look about or gawk,
    Little Mouse!
    In the wood is your deep

    tunnel where you are safe to sleep
    in a nest of leaves, but do not walk!
    You'd better **L E A P**

    Now, before the silent sweep
    of Mr. Owl; before his talons lock
    up a little wood-mouse for keeps.

L E A P Little Mouse
L - - E - - A - - P -

Villanelle

Napaeozapus insignis

The Woodland Jumping Mouse usually walks, but when he is in a hurry (like when an owl is after him) he can make huge leaps. He is only 8-10 inches long including his tail, but he can cover eight feet in **one** jump. That's twelve times his own size. If you could jump twelve times your own size, you'd be down the block in a couple of hops!

Porcupine

She lumbered in the dark,
    seemingly at ease
      despite approaching barks.
And it must be said —
    she tried to warn him.
Turned to show the skunk-like
    stripe down her back.
Puffed her cheeks and
    chattered through her teeth.
But he was young,
    excitable and dumb!
She raised her quills…
He rushed in willy-nilly,
    then beat his retreat in an
    agony of howls.
For her, a slow climb
    up the nearest tree.
For him, a most unpleasant
    visit to the vet.

Free verse

Erethizon dorsatum

Porcupine quills are mostly hollow, with downward-pointing scales at the tips, like the barb on a fishhook. When Porcupine slaps with her tail, the quills easily come loose from her skin and burrow into the victim. Quills are difficult and painful to remove. However, porcupines would rather escape up a tree than use their quills, and most animals learn to leave them alone.

Hoary Bats

All the lady Hoary bats,
Hazel, Hilda, Helen, Rhoda,
pack their bags, put on their hats
and fly up north to Minnesota.

Every summer renting cabins,
catching moths beneath the moon,
knitting tiny batty booties
for the babies born in June.

All the Hoary boy bats,
Harry, Henry, Hank, and Bob,
stay behind in Arizona
working on their summer job.

Then, Hazel, Hilda, Helen, Rhoda,
bring the kids, out-fly the snow,
join the guys across the border,
munching moths in Mexico.

Lasiurus cinereus

Hoary means frosty, and Hoary Bats have white-tipped hair that looks frosted. Scientists are trying to learn more about these bats, because they are different than most other kinds. Most bats roost in attics or caves, in large groups. But Hoary Bats roost individually — in trees! Scientists are also studying their migration patterns and feeding habits. Bats are very helpful mammals, because they eat so many bugs. How would you like to be a bat scientist?

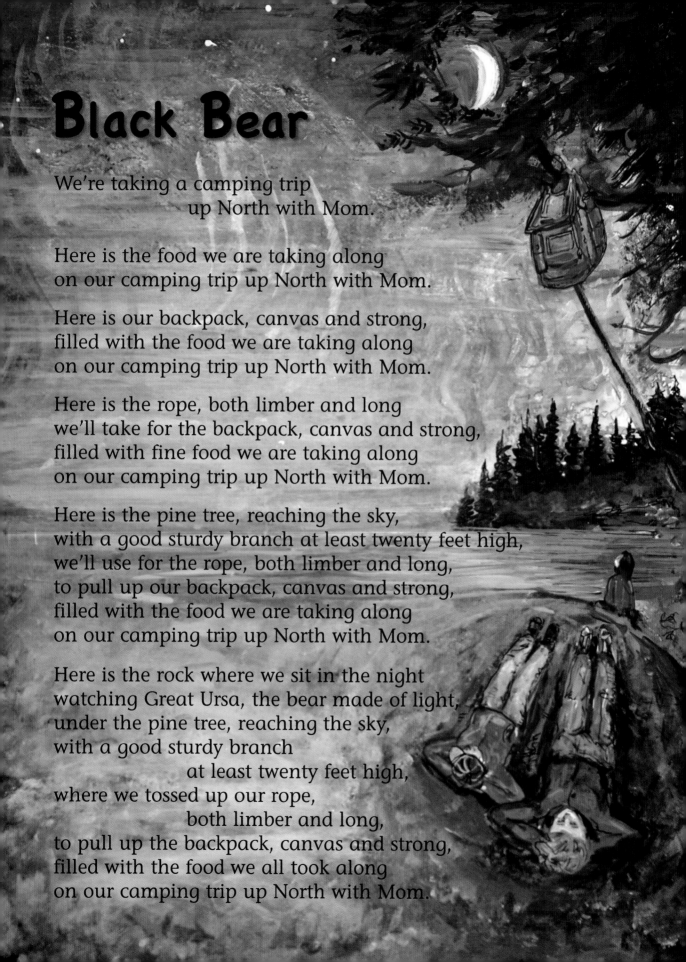

Black Bear

We're taking a camping trip
           up North with Mom.

Here is the food we are taking along
on our camping trip up North with Mom.

Here is our backpack, canvas and strong,
filled with the food we are taking along
on our camping trip up North with Mom.

Here is the rope, both limber and long
we'll take for the backpack, canvas and strong,
filled with fine food we are taking along
on our camping trip up North with Mom.

Here is the pine tree, reaching the sky,
with a good sturdy branch at least twenty feet high,
we'll use for the rope, both limber and long,
to pull up our backpack, canvas and strong,
filled with the food we are taking along
on our camping trip up North with Mom.

Here is the rock where we sit in the night
watching Great Ursa, the bear made of light,
under the pine tree, reaching the sky,
with a good sturdy branch
                  at least twenty feet high,
where we tossed up our rope,
                  both limber and long,
to pull up the backpack, canvas and strong,
filled with the food we all took along
on our camping trip up North with Mom.

Here's a big mess, all scattered around!
And here are the big muddy tracks that we found
criss-crossing the rock where we sat in the night,
watching Great Ursa, the bear made of light,
under the pine tree, reaching the sky
with a good sturdy branch
                              at least twenty feet high,
where we tossed up our rope,
                              both limber and long,
and pulled up our backpack, canvas and strong,
that *was* filled with food to last all week long
on our camping trip up North with Mom!

Cumulative poem

Ursus americanus

Black Bears are a popular symbol of the North Woods. They are omnivores, feasting on berries, twigs, leaf buds, grubs, small mammals, fish, and honey … if they can find a hive.

Black Bears are naturally shy and will usually run away if they hear people in the forest. However, if they get used to eating food from garbage cans and campsites, even Black Bears may become dangerous. So do Ursus and yourself a big favor — DO NOT FEED THE BEARS!

White-tailed Deer

On the road out to our shack
a large buck raised his head,
crowned with a twelve-point rack.
"Like a king!" I said.

The large buck raised his head,
for a moment standing tall.
"Like a king!" I said …
then he wasn't there at all!

For a moment he stood tall
and flashed his tail-flag,
then he wasn't there at all,
that beautiful young stag.

He flashed his tail-flag
and raised his twelve-point rack,
that beautiful young stag
on the road out to our shack.

Pantoum

Odocoileus virginianus

White-tailed Deer are a common sight along roadways. In the winter, they gather in large herds led by a female. Moving in a group helps keep trails open through deep snow and provides protection from predators. In the north country, deer hunting is a popular sport and venison is a popular food.

Northern Flying Squirrel

They glide through the air
with the greatest of ease,
the fine Flying Squirrels
dropping down from the trees.
They spread out their legs
and hang on the breeze,
and sing as they sail away.

They glide tree to tree
and they float to the ground,
the envy of every
Gray Squirrel around.
Moreover they make
a most marvelous sound,
for they sing as they sail away.

Lyric — to the tune of "The Daring Young Man on the Flying Trapeze"

Glaucomys sabrinus

A Northern Flying Squirrel can glide through the air almost
the distance of a football field, but it does not actually fly
like a bird or a bat. You might be able to hear the Flying
Squirrels' chirping, bird-like sounds. However, they mostly
come out after dark, so they're hard to see. Find a dead
tree with woodpecker holes near the top, then tap on it.
If a Flying Squirrel is nesting there, she might poke her
head out to see who's knocking.

Kodiak

Ursus arctos middendorffii

Kodiaks are the biggest bears in the world. They feast on salmon that are swimming up the rivers to their spawning pools, but most of their diet consists of roots, berries, leaves and buds. Many tourists travel to Alaska to view the mighty Kodiak Bears ... from a safe distance.

Oh Kodiak! How awful are your claws,
like scimitars of gleaming ivory!
And fearsome are the teeth within your jaws!
You cast a ten-foot shadow over me,
rising from the river's rugged bank.
And huddled in the crevice of this rock,
I smell your dripping fur, all dark and dank.
Petrified, my knees begin to knock!
Then down you plunge into the river's wake,
with silver salmon running deep beneath,
and make your paws into a living rake,
to sweep the fish into your waiting teeth.

Oh what a tale I'll tell when I get back …
of how I faced the mighty Kodiak!

Sonnet

Otter

Otters are an oddity of nature,
  I would say.
They seem to think
  that everything
    is an excuse to play.
When winter comes
  and snow falls deep
    and other creatures go to sleep,
The otters just make snow-slides;
  they're good at making snow-slides;
    they love to dive down snow-slides,
      slippery and steep.

    Otters don't mind freezing wind,
      though all the ground is icing.
    It simply makes tobogganing
      that much more enticing.
    When cold spring rains make others shake,
      and all that mud is hard to take,
      The otters just make mud-slides,
        smooshy, mooshy mud-slides;
          they love to slip down mud-slides,
          right into the lake.

River Otters may be the world's most playful animal. Family members play together, but if no one is around, a River Otter will play alone. They really do make slides of mud, ice, or snow. They take a running start, tuck their forelegs back and *Lontra* shoot down as though tobogganing. River *canadensis* Otters also can swim rapidly underwater, forward and backward, looking like torpedoes. We need clean lakes and rivers to keep otters healthy.

You

Yes, **YOU**!
You're a mammal too.
You have warm blood,
and you have hair,
and other traits that mammals share.
You are a person,
it is true ...
but you're a mammal too!

Homo sapiens

Homo sapiens means wise man, or woman, or child. And you are definitely a mammal. Mammals have hair or fur, are warm-blooded, and mothers are able to nurse their young. Humans have all three of these traits.

We share another trait unique to mammals — our middle ears have three tiny, moveable bones that transmit sound. Next time your parents tell you to stop acting like a wild animal, remind them that you ARE a mammal, after all!

Winter's Nap

When golden leaves scatter and
branches are bare.
When frost diamonds glitter and
sparkle the air,
It's time for sleep,
It's time for sleep;

When Bear seeks her den and the geese have all flown,
And Deermouse curls tight in his snug burrow home,
Not making a peep,
Not even a peep;

When Northern lights dance with a cold silver moon,
And blizzards sweep in with a wild banshee tune,
And snow lies deep,
It piles so deep;

Then warm flannel nightgowns are buttoned up tight,
And embers will glow in the wood stove all night.
The cocoa is drunk and the last story told,
And deep downy covers will keep out the cold.
    It's time for sleep.
    Now go to sleep,
    Go safely and softly to sleep.

Lullaby

ZZZzzzzz

Mammals of the north have to survive long, cold winters. Sleep
is one way for animals to conserve energy. Some mammals, like
Jumping Mice, truly hibernate. Others, like squirrels, sleep on
the very coldest days and are active when the weather
warms. Even Black Bears do not truly hibernate, but their
breathing and heartbeat slow way down. They make a
den and take a long winter's nap. Deer and moose
rest right on the snow. Aren't you glad for a
snug warm bed? Good-night!

In memory of my Dad.   —C.S.D

In memory of my Grandpa
and to all who pushed and guided me. —A.H.

ABOUT THE AUTHOR

Cheryl Dannenbring enjoyed sharing poetry with her elementary students for more than thirty years. After retiring, she combined her interest in poetry for children with her love of the North Woods to write Beaver, Bear, Snowshoe Hare. Cheryl lives in Duluth with her husband, Walt, and one large, fluffy cat named Jasper.

ABOUT THE ARTIST

Anna Hess lives on the North Shore of Lake Superior among many of the mammals in this book. She loves observing them in their natural habitat, finding humor in their world, and portraying them in a whimsical way to add fun to our world. Anna enjoys illustrating as a perfect union of language and visual art. Her work is displayed at Last Chance Gallery.

Text © 2009 by Cheryl Dannenbring
Illustrations © 2009 by Anna Hess

Printed in Minnesota
United States of America
Corporate Graphics, N. Mankato, MN
10 9 8 7 6 5 4 3 2 1   082009

Published February, 2010 by
Raven Productions, Inc.
P.O. Box 188, Ely, MN 55731
218-365-3375
www.ravenwords.com

Library of Congress Cataloging-in-Publication Data

Dannenbring, Cheryl.
 Beaver, bear, snowshoe hare : mammal poems / by Cheryl Dannenbring ; illustrations by Anna Hess.
  p. cm.
 ISBN 978-0-9819307-0-1 (hardcover : alk. paper) -- ISBN 978-0-9819307-1-8 (softcover : alk. paper)
 1. Mammals--North America--Juvenile literature. 2. Mammals--North America--Pictorial works. 3. Mammals--North America--Juvenile poetry. I. Hess, Anna, ill. II. Title.
 QL715.D36 2009
 599.097--dc22

All rights reserved. No part of this book may be reproduced or transmitted in any form or by any means without prior written permission from the publisher except for brief excerpts in reviews.